CHAPTER ONE

THE MASK OF AH PUCH

DRRRRRRRR! A tall, powerful drill cut
through the dry, dusty earth of a Texas oil
field, searching for some more of the gloopy
black liquid. Three men stood by it, operating
the controls, the sweltering sun almost melting
them in their heavy protective overalls.

EEEEEEEEEK! Suddenly, the drill let out
an ear-shattering squeal. The men stepped back
as hot smoke began to billow up from the hole
in the ground. Something was wrong.

The ground at their feet began to move.
Small cracks – barely larger than spiders –
appeared in the rocky soil. They grew quickly,
spreading out in all directions, churning the

ground into rubble. Something was *definitely* wrong!

The oil rig workers ran, leaping hurriedly over the cracks appearing before them, trying to get to safety. Huge swirling clouds of dust and sand whipped at them as they fled.

At last, with a deafening **CREEEAK** of metal, the enormous drill toppled down into the gaping hole that had opened up below it. It clanked noisily as it sank down into the darkness, and then a spooky silence fell over the area.

It didn't last long. As the workers crept up

to the edge of the hole for a closer look, a pillar of flame exploded from within it. The column of fire stretched up to the sky, punching clean through the clouds.

The workers watched on, numb with shock as the flames flickered and danced. For a moment, they could have sworn the fire twisted to form an ugly, terrifying face.

Then, a final rush of wind snuffed the fire out as quickly as it had started. In the silence that followed, everyone heard the faint **PLOP** of something hitting the ground. They stepped closer to the fallen object and stared. It stared back.

A mask – its features frozen in an evil scowl – lay on the rock. For a second, its eyes glowed an eerie shade of green.

The drill had struck *something* – but it definitely wasn't oil!

❉ ❉ ❉

At The Rust Bucket's small dining table, Ben and Gwen munched on a sample of Grandpa's latest recipe. It tasted . . . OK. Better than his usual stuff, anyway. Grandpa himself had already finished one bowl and was now well into his second helping.

'Well,' he asked them, 'what do you think?'

The cousins glanced down at their bowls. It was still too early to give their final verdict.

'What's the crunchy stuff?' asked Ben.

'Dung beetles,' replied his grandfather.

Ben and Gwen spat the food back into

their bowls and hurriedly scraped their tongues with their fingernails. Why couldn't they just have a *normal* meal for once? Would it kill Grandpa to cook a burger?

'What?' the old man asked, smirking. 'Too spicy?' He watched them retching in disgust. 'You'll get used to it.'

A piercing alarm screeched from The Rust Bucket's hidden speakers, startling everyone to attention. Above Grandpa's head, a flat-screen monitor unfolded from a concealed compartment and lowered itself down.

Grandpa Max's face went a deathly shade of pale when his eyes fixed on the screen. He leaned closer to the object on the monitor and stared.

It stared back.

'No,' he gasped, his eyes fixed on the glowing green eyes of an all-too-familiar mask.

Gwen and Ben exchanged a worried glance. They'd never seen Grandpa look so scared before.

'Grandpa,' asked Ben. 'What is it?'

'The Mask of Ah Puch,' he replied gravely. He turned the screen so his grandchildren could see for themselves. 'It's the key to the most powerful and destructive weapon ever created.'

Pushing the monitor away, Grandpa Max left the table and slid into the driving seat. Ben scrambled to take his place up front as The Rust Bucket spluttered into life.

'The Mask of Ah Puch is the key to the Sword of Ek Chuah,' Grandpa explained, powering the motorhome along a narrow dusty track. 'The Plumbers searched for it for decades without any luck.'

'Ek Chuah?' Ben frowned. 'What kind of alien is that?'

The windscreen of The Rust Bucket shimmered for a moment before a holographic projection of a map swam into focus. A red light appeared on it, blinking, pinpointing the location of the mask.

'Not alien, *Mayan*,' Grandpa corrected. 'Ek Chuah was the Mayan God of War. His sword was rumoured to have levelled whole cities with just one swipe.'

'Ha! Sounds like just the kind of thing the world's most powerful ten-year-old should have,' said Ben, smirking.

'This is no toy, Benjamin,' his grandfather snapped. The tone of his voice made Ben and Gwen jump in their seats. 'Whoever controls the sword controls the destiny of mankind, and I will *not* let it fall into the wrong hands!'

❈ ❈ ❈

Half an hour later, The Rust Bucket pulled into the oil field. It crept up to the main office building, where the tracking device told Grandpa the mask was being kept.

Watched closely by suspicious security

guards, Grandpa Max cut the engine and joined his grandchildren in the back of the motorhome.

'Bet they're keeping it in the basement,' he mumbled to himself. 'Ben, you go alien and sneak in, then open the side door for us.'

'"Sneak in"? Don't you mean *break* in?' suggested Ben.

Grandpa fixed him with an icy glare. 'I haven't the time to explain how important it is for us to get the mask,' he said. 'Now, can I count on you or not?'

'You know you can, Grandpa.' Ben nodded, a little hurt by the way his grandfather was speaking to him.

Without a word, Grandpa Max nodded back, and went to wait up front.

'What's up with Grandpa?' Ben whispered to his cousin. 'He's so . . . *intense.*'

'Cut him some slack, will you?' Gwen replied. 'He's trying to save the world!'

Ben adjusted the dial on the face of the

Omnitrix. Saving the world was his speciality! He slammed his hand down on the watch. Immediately, the cloud of swirling green wrapped round him, altering his DNA.

Ben's pinkish skin grew grey as stone as his entire body began to shrink. His eyes grew bulgy, until they stuck out from his head like two blinking green bubbles. When it came to sneaking into places, not many of his aliens could beat the tiny Grey Matter!

Gwen opened the door of The Rust Bucket just wide enough for him to slip out. After a

quick check to make sure the coast was clear, Grey Matter hopped down from the motorhome and scampered up a drainpipe fixed to the office-building wall.

Inside The Rust Bucket, Gwen and Grandpa watched him go.

'I know Ben can be a major doofus,' Gwen said. 'But don't you think you were a little –'

'You're just kids,' interrupted Grandpa. 'I don't expect you to understand.'

Gwen bit her bottom lip and looked away. Ben was right – their grandfather had *never* acted like this before.

❈ ❈ ❈

On the bathroom floor of the office building, a round metal drain cover rose a few centimetres into the air. With a grunt, Grey Matter pushed his way through, before letting the cover slip back over the hole.

The little alien groaned when he realised a large blob of chewing gum had got stuck to his head somewhere along his journey.

'Oh, man,' he complained, 'I should've just gone Cannonbolt and *busted* my way in!'

He flicked the chewing gum away, then stopped. A warm breeze had suddenly begun to blow against the back of his neck. If he listened closely, he could also make out a slow, regular wheezing. It sounded almost exactly like . . . *breathing*!

Grey Matter spun round, then gulped down a mouthful of panic. A German Shepherd dog loomed over him, its gums pulled back to expose two rows of sharp, yellowing teeth.

He backed away, only to hear a growling from the other direction. Turning, his worst fears were confirmed. There were two of the dogs – and they were coming right for him!

CHAPTER TWO

THE FOREVER KNIGHTS

As the dogs leaped, so did Grey Matter. The alien sprang upwards on his frog-like legs, just as the two crazed canines pounced. Both dogs gave a yelp of pain when their heads knocked together with a hollow **THWOCK!**

Grey Matter scurried for the bathroom door, rushing to get away before the stunned mutts came back to their senses. As he scampered through the door, he hurried back out and heaved it closed behind him, trapping the animals inside.

'Ha!' the alien cried, listening to their frenzied barking. 'Who's the big dog now?'

❈ ❈ ❈

By the side wall of the office building, away from the prying eyes of the security guards, Grandpa Max impatiently tapped his foot. There was a narrow hatchway here, leading down into the building's basement area. Ben should have opened it up by now. What was keeping the boy?

The door handle gave a **CLUNK** and swung open. Grey Matter hopped out, ready to be congratulated on a job well done.

'About time,' Grandpa muttered. Grey Matter watched sadly as Grandpa Max trudged on down the stairs, not saying another word.

Gwen reached down and picked the tiny alien up by the back of his shirt. She sniffed him cautiously before screwing up her face in disgust.

'Ewww!' she winced. 'Why do you smell like dog slobber?'

Carrying Grey Matter on her shoulder, Gwen descended the steps behind her grandfather, being careful to leave the door unlocked behind her.

❈ ❈ ❈

Up above, unnoticed by any of the Tennysons, a black car with darkened windows drew up next to The Rust Bucket.

❈ ❈ ❈

Grandpa Max marched along the basement corridor, searching for any sign of the mask. Behind him, Gwen raced to keep up, Grey Matter holding on to her ear for dear life.

'Have you ever seen Grandpa this serious?' Gwen whispered.

Grey Matter shook his head. 'I've never seen *anyone* this serious!'

Grandpa threw open a door and stepped into a small office. A desk and chair stood in one corner. Next to them was a large, cast-iron safe.

'It *has* to be in here,' he said.

'I'm on it!' cried Grey Matter. The super-genius alien hopped on to the safe and pressed his ear against the solid door. With one foot, he twirled the dial of the locking mechanism, listening for the clicks that would tell him the lock pins were falling into place.

In just a few seconds, the door swung open.

'Good job, Ben!' said Gwen.

Grandpa didn't speak. Instead, he pulled the door fully open. A faint gasp escaped his lips as his eyes fell on the contents of the safe.

'Beautiful, isn't it?' he said. Gwen and Grey Matter peered in at the hideous mask.

'Ah, not exactly . . .' shrugged the little grey alien.

Grandpa Max picked up the mask, his hands trembling. He stared into the empty eye sockets, as if hypnotised by them.

'Over forty years of searching,' he mumbled, 'and now, finally, you're –'

'I thought you'd retired from the plumbing business, Mr Tennyson,' boomed a voice from behind the group. They turned to find three men blocking the doorway, their faces obscured by expressionless metal masks. The lead man stepped forward. 'Or may I call you Max?'

Grey Matter's eyes narrowed. They'd encountered these guys already during the summer. They were bad news.

'It's Enoch and those Forever Knight guys who tried to slice and dice me!' he hissed.

'How nice of you to remember,' spat Enoch. 'And, of course, how can I forget the family who left the Forever Knights without a castle?'

'Whatever happened you brought upon yourselves,' scowled Grandpa Max.

'Aren't we the feisty sewer rat?' drawled Enoch. 'I'd love to chat about old times, but I'm late for holding the world at my mercy, so I'll be taking that mask now.'

Grandpa Max narrowed his eyes. 'Over my dead body.'

'Excellent suggestion,' chuckled Enoch. He gestured to his two henchmen. 'Gentlemen . . .'

In unison, the two masked villains drew their swords. The blades cracked and crackled with an electric-blue glow.

'Hey, what's going on here?' A security guard blundered through the door behind the Forever Knights, completely unaware of what he was about to get himself into.

Taking advantage of the distraction, Grey Matter sprang at Enoch, draping himself over the villain's eyes like a blindfold.

'Run!' he shouted, clinging on tightly.

Grandpa and Gwen didn't need telling twice. The Mask of Ah Puch clasped tightly under Grandpa Max's arm, they dodged past the knights and shoulder-barged the security guard out into the hallway.

'We've got burglars,' yelled the guard into his walkie-talkie. 'Seal the exits!'

Enoch roared and tore the squirming Grey Matter off his mask. With a flick of his wrist, he sent the alien spinning across the room before the three knights set off in pursuit of Grandpa and Gwen.

Grey Matter hit the top of the desk and skidded across its surface, sliding closer and closer to the edge. As his feet slipped off the desktop, the bug-eyed alien twisted and threw out his arms. His stick-like hands caught hold of a bundle of papers. His body slammed hard against the side of the table – **THUNK!** – but still he hung on.

Below him lay the sharp metal jaws of a paper shredder. If he fell on to them, they'd whir into life, chopping him into hundreds of little squidgy bits.

'No way I'm winding up as alien

coleslaw!' he said, pressing his feet against the side of the desk. With a heave, he launched himself backwards, flipped twice in the air, then landed safely on the office floor. Grey Matter allowed himself a brief smile. If he ever gave up crime-fighting, he could always start a career as a gymnast!

�֍ �֍ ✖

Grandpa rushed up a flight of metal stairs, taking them two at a time. Gwen hurried along behind. For an old man, her grandfather sure could move when he wanted to!

At the top of the stairs, Grandpa Max pulled back. Two security guards stood by the exit, their backs to the Tennysons.

'Wrong way,' Grandpa hissed, changing direction. He led Gwen towards a set of wide double doors, which he hoped would lead them outside.

Suddenly, Grandpa felt the mask slip from his grasp. He whipped round, clawing at the air, desperately trying to catch it. It was no use. A high-tech grappling hook had snared the mask, and was pulling it back to the waiting Enoch.

'Your loss is my gain,' sneered the knight as he and his two companions turned and fled.

A shadow began to fall across Grandpa and Gwen. They turned to see a thick metal shutter lowering down in front of the door. If they didn't move fast, they'd be trapped!

'Grab on,' Grandpa barked, catching Gwen by the hand. Side by side, they sprinted for the exit. The shutter was almost fully closed. This was going to be a tight squeeze!

Throwing themselves to the floor, Grandpa Max and Gwen slid beneath the steel shutter. The sharp metal bottom brushed against Grandpa's bulging belly, but they made it through just before it clanged fully closed.

❈ ❈ ❈

Outside, a grey shape dropped from the mouth of a drainage pipe. It screamed and flapped its arms as it plummeted down into a dumpster full of rotting garbage.

In a bright flash of red, a full-sized Ben found himself sitting among the rubbish. Flies buzzed around him, and crawled across a mouldy banana skin balanced on his head like a particularly smelly hat.

Ben grimaced. 'I hate it when this happens.'

The Rust Bucket's brakes squealed to a stop just in front of him. 'We don't have time to fool around, Ben,' Grandpa bellowed. 'Get in!'

Ben clambered free of the mound of garbage and jumped into The Rust Bucket. Even before the door was closed, Grandpa slammed the vehicle into reverse and screeched out of the car park. The Forever

Knights had the Mask of Ah Puch, *and* they had a head start. If they weren't caught, they could find the Sword of Ek Chuah, and then the world would be theirs for the taking!

CHAPTER THREE

HIGH-SPEED PURSUIT

Asleek, black sedan car sped along a Texan track, spraying up clouds of dust in its wake. In the back seat, Enoch studied the Mask of Ah Puch, all the while laughing the laugh of a madman. He had found the mask. Soon all the power in the world would be his!

Up in front, one of Enoch's two guards glanced in the rear-view mirror. His eyes narrowed behind his mask as he tried to make out the shape of the large object tearing along the track behind them. His hands tightened on the wheel when he realised The Rust Bucket was closing on them fast.

But not fast enough for Grandpa Max.

Flicking a switch on the dashboard, he activated the motorhome's turbo mode. The hidden jet engines clicked into place, and a powerful blast of flame sent the vehicle rocketing along the road.

CLANG! The front of The Rust Bucket slammed hard against the back of the Forever Knights' car. Inside, Enoch was bounced around wildly in his leather seat.

The masked villain's fingers flew to a control panel mounted into the back of the seat in front. At the touch of a screen, the boot of the car sprang open and a spinning saw blade lashed out, cutting a deep scar into the front of The Rust Bucket. Grandpa was forced to pull back before the blade cut clean through the motorhome's engine.

'Come on,' cried Gwen, giving her cousin a nudge. 'Wildmutt? Ripjaws? *Somebody?*'

Ben frantically spun the dial on the Omnitrix. It glowed red – not yet recharged enough to spring back into life.

'I'm trying,' Ben protested, 'but the stupid watch won't let me!'

In the driver's seat, Grandpa Max reached a decision. 'This is a job for a Plumber,' he announced, before pushing a button on the steering wheel.

'Auto-driver engaged,' stated a computer voice from somewhere behind the dashboard.

Without a word, Grandpa swivelled in his chair, walked to the back of The Rust Bucket, and locked himself in the toilet. Ben and Gwen stared at the door to the small wooden cubicle in stunned silence.

At last, Ben gave a shrug. 'Well,' he said, 'I guess when you gotta go, you gotta go.'

❈ ❈ ❈

In the car in front, Enoch had turned his attention back to the Mask of Ah Puch. He turned it over in his hands, letting the light streaming in through the sunroof catch the mask's emerald-green eyes. As the sun's rays struck them, they became twin beams of power. Enoch watched the beams combine to form something wondrous.

'Excellent!' he crowed, his own eyes sparkling like stars beneath his metal faceplate. The mask worked, just as the legends had said! It had told him where to find the sword. There would be no stopping him now!

�֎ ✖ ✖

The door to The Rust Bucket's tiny toilet flew open. Grandpa stepped from inside, no longer wearing his familiar orange Hawaiian shirt. Instead, he was kitted out in the grey boiler suit and body armour of a Plumber.

'Uh, Grandpa . . .' Ben frowned. 'What's with the fashion show?'

'It's my Plumber suit,' his grandfather replied. 'Been saving it for the right time.' He glanced through the side window. The Forever Knights' car was right alongside them. 'Like now,' he finished.

Taking two magnetic pads from his belt and slipping them over his hands, Grandpa pulled open the door of the motorhome. He calculated the distance between the two vehicles carefully. The suit was tight and he wasn't as fit as he'd been last time he wore it, but he was still fairly sure he could make the jump.

With a grunt of effort, Grandpa Max hurled himself on to the top of the knights' car. He skidded across the roof, looking certain to slide off the other side. At the last moment, he slammed the magnetic pads down on to the roof. They stuck fast to the metal, holding him in place.

Gritting his teeth, Grandpa crawled across the roof of the long car, towards the open sunroof. He was so fixated on getting the mask back, he didn't notice the two eerie figures standing on top of The Rust Bucket. The Forever Knights cracked their knuckles menacingly. The Plumbers weren't the only ones to have auto-driver mode on their vehicles!

Grandpa edged closer to the sunroof and peered inside. There was the mask, sitting by itself on a seat! He gave a sigh of relief. This must be his lucky day!

SSSSSHCK! A shimmering blue blade tore through the roof of the car, narrowly missing Grandpa's head. The old man rolled on to his left side, moments before the blade stabbed back up through the space where he'd just been.

The sword sliced up a third time, forcing Grandpa to roll all the way off the roof. He hung on with one hand, the metal toes of his boots scraping along the ground, sending showers of sparks up behind the car.

'Grandpa!' cried Gwen, who was watching the scene from inside The Rust Bucket. Spurred on by the sound of his granddaughter's voice, Grandpa Max began dragging himself back up on to the roof of the speeding car.

Suddenly, a tall dark figure swung in through The Rust Bucket's open door. Gwen screamed at the sight of the Forever Knight, then ducked under his arm as he made a grab at her.

'You want a fight?' Ben bellowed from the front of the vehicle. 'Try picking on someone your own size!'

The knight drew his blazing blue sword and lunged at him, but the boy rolled out of attacking range. Spinning round, the masked villain raised the sword a second time and advanced. Ben glanced down at the Omnitrix. Still red. Still useless. There was no escaping this time. He was done for!

THWACK! The door of the motorhome's small fridge flew open, smacking the knight in the face. He staggered backwards towards the motorhome's side door, stunned by the blow. Ben glanced up at his cousin, who stood next to the fridge, giving him a thumbs-up.

Acting quickly, Ben snatched up a cast-iron cooking pot. It still contained half the meal Grandpa had made for them earlier. Ben grinned. Time to get rid of two problems at once!

Twirling his arm round, Ben launched the pot at the knight. It hit him like a cannonball to the chest. His arms waving about wildly, the villain toppled backwards through the door, where he bounced hard on the hot tarmac road.

'Nice job!' cried Ben and Gwen, giving each other a high five. Their celebrations didn't last long, however. With a splintering crash, the motorhome's sunroof exploded inwards. Through the hole they could make out the shape of the second knight.

Snatching up the fire extinguisher, Gwen rushed over to the shattered sunroof. She pointed the nozzle up through the gap in the ceiling and let rip with the chemical spray.

The cloud of choking gas seeped

in through the gaps in the knight's mask, blinding him and choking him at the same time. Coughing and spluttering, he stepped backwards and slipped off the roof. Screaming, he tumbled all the way off the road bridge they were travelling across, hitting the water below with a distant **SPLASH**.

Grandpa Max was back on the roof of Enoch's car, but he didn't know how long for. The blade of the sword had turned the metal into something resembling Swiss cheese, and still Enoch continued to stab at him.

An idea struck him. As the blue blade swished up at him for what felt like the fiftieth time, Grandpa attached one of the magnetic pads to it. The pad wedged against the roof, making it impossible for Enoch to pull the sword back through.

Inside the car, Enoch growled. He pulled with all his strength, but the sword was well and truly stuck. The knight glanced down at the seat next to him. At least he still had . . .

The mask! Where was the mask? Enoch stood up and stuck his head out through the sunroof. Over in The Rust Bucket doorway, Grandpa Max held up the Mask of Ah Puch. He gave Enoch a wink, then stepped inside, pulling the door shut behind him.

Relieved to have the mask back, Grandpa clambered back into the driver's seat of his beloved motorhome. His blood ran cold when he looked out through the front window; an enormous truck was heading straight towards them!

Grandpa tried to swerve, but Enoch's car blocked The Rust Bucket's escape. The truck was close, and getting closer by the second. Soon, there would be no escape. Any second now, they were going to crash!

CHAPTER FOUR

THE TEMPLE OF EK CHUAH

'**H**old on!' Grandpa barked. He pressed another button and yet more jet engines unfolded from within The Rust Bucket. The motorhome sped up rapidly, rocketing towards the oncoming truck.

The rocket boosters took it soaring past Enoch's car. Grandpa twisted the steering hard to the right. The sudden turn forced The Rust Bucket up on to just three of its six wheels. The truck blared its horn as it thundered past, just centimetres from the teetering motorhome.

When they were safely past the eighteen-wheeler, Grandpa Max wrenched the wheel again, bringing The Rust Bucket back down on to all six wheels. A stunned Enoch could only watch as a hatch opened in the back of the speeding motorhome, and hundreds of spiky metal balls spilled out on to the road.

BANG! BANG! BANG! BANG! The tyres on Enoch's car burst instantly and the vehicle skidded to a clumsy stop in the middle of the road. The knight punched a number into his mobile phone as he watched the motorhome flee. The phone rang twice before it was answered.

'Send in the bird,' hissed Enoch.

A few miles further along the road, a bright-red warning light blinked on the dashboard of The Rust Bucket. With a cough and a wheeze, the turbo boosters shuddered to a stop. The motorhome slowed gradually before coming to a halt, clouds of steam rising from the overheated engine.

Grandpa dug his toolbox out from under the driver's seat, stomped outside and began the job of figuring out what had caused the engine to fail.

Gwen and Ben stepped down behind him, Ben clutching the Mask of Ah Puch in his hands. He turned it over, studying the gruesome-looking object. It didn't *look* all that special – just creepy, really.

As the eyes of the mask caught the sun's rays, they began to glow a bright green. Ben gulped nervously as twin beams of emerald light projected from the eye sockets and down on to the dusty ground.

'Uh . . . Grandpa?'

'Not now, Ben,' snapped his grandfather, still busy tinkering with the engine.

'I think you're gonna want to see this,' Ben insisted.

Sighing, Grandpa Max turned to his grandson. He gasped at what he saw. The mask was projecting a holographic image of an ancient Mayan temple. It looked almost real enough to touch.

'It's the map to the ancient Mayan temple of Ek Chuah,' said Grandpa. A horrible thought suddenly struck him. If Ben had been able to find the map so easily, then that meant Enoch probably had too!

Grandpa dropped his tools. There was no time to lose. He looked at Ben and nodded towards the Omnitrix. 'We need to beat them to that temple!'

�֎ ✖ ✖

Stinkfly buzzed low over an ancient South American jungle, struggling to stay in the air. It had taken a long time to fly this far, mostly because he'd had to carry Grandpa and Gwen the whole way. Gwen he could manage, but Grandpa really could do with losing some weight!

'Can't you go any faster?' his grandfather demanded.

'I'm sorry, Grandpa,' Stinkfly replied. 'I'm not used to flying with passengers.'

His four alien eyes squinted. Up ahead, he could make out the top of the temple. They were getting close. Just as well, because the Omnitrix had started to flash, and any moment now they would all –

They screamed as they fell. High, twisting branches clawed at them, slowing them down, saving them from becoming pancakes on the jungle floor. With a **THUD! THUD! THUD!** all three of them hit the ground. Ben spat out a mouthful of leaves he'd collected on the way down.

'Man –' he winced –'I really need to work on my emergency landings.'

Grandpa Max paused in the foliage near the temple. A black helicopter stood silently next to the ancient ruins. The Forever Knights were already here. Peering through the trees, he could see the villains. They were trying to blow open the temple doors with dynamite, but weren't having any luck.

Keeping low, Grandpa led Gwen and Ben up towards the far side of the temple. He studied the wall. Its giant bricks had been carved from solid rock. There was no way they could break through.

'There's always a secret entrance to these temples,' Grandpa Max muttered. He pushed a few of the stones. 'Where *is* it?'

Ben unclipped the mask from his grandfather's belt. He held it up over his face and peered through the eyeholes.

'Ben, what are you doing?' Grandpa demanded.

'If this thing could show us how to get this far, maybe it can show us how to get in.'

Ben slowly turned his gaze across the wall. Aside from everything having a faint green tint, it all looked pretty much normal.

Wait! He backtracked along the bricks. One of the stone blocks seemed to be giving off a faint yellow glow. Ben stepped forwards and touched the brick. At once, a hidden doorway slid open before him, and Ben, Gwen and Grandpa Max stepped inside.

The temple smelled of damp and death. The faint glow from the sun outside was the only source of light as they hurried along a narrow stone corridor.

'The sword would be kept in the centre of the temple, on the lowest floor,' Grandpa announced. 'There should be some stairs nearby.'

'Stairs?' Ben winced. 'Where's the express elevator when you really need it?'

The darkness enveloped them now, making it impossible to see. Grandpa felt along the wall for a torch. When he found one, he lit it using a spark from a fire-lighting device on his Plumber suit. The torch burst into a bright-orange ball of flame in his hand.

Ben looked down and realised his toes were poking over the edge of an enormous drop. Shocked, he lost his balance and began to topple forward. He span his arms in wide circles, desperately trying to straighten up, but it was no use. He was going to fall!

A strong hand caught him by the belt of his trousers. Ben breathed a sigh of relief when Grandpa heaved him back up to safety.

'Whew, that was close,' breathed Grandpa Max. 'Almost lost the mask!'

'OK,' whispered Gwen as their grandfather set off towards the stairs. 'Would you say obsessed?'

Ben nodded. 'Once he gets that sword, he'll be himself again, right?'

Gwen could only shrug. The way Grandpa was acting, there was no saying if he'd ever be himself again.

✸ ✸ ✸

Ben wheezed as they finally arrived at one of the lower levels of the temple. Grandpa was already there, studying a carved stone that stood in the middle of the room. The indent on top of it looked to be a perfect match for the Mask of Ah Puch.

'This is it,' said Grandpa Max. He held the mask above the stone. Finally, after all these years, he would –

'Who says you can't get a Plumber when you need one?' cackled Enoch, as he stepped from the shadows. Two Forever Knights raced forward and snatched Ben and Gwen. They struggled, but the knights were too strong. 'Without you bringing the mask,' continued Enoch, 'we wouldn't have been able to get inside the great chamber.'

Grandpa felt like crying out. How could he have been so stupid? Whatever happened next would be all his fault!

He was too consumed by guilt to notice Enoch prise the mask from his fingers. The leader of the knights spent a few seconds admiring the prize he had worked so hard to win.

Enoch walked slowly across to the other side of the room and stopped by a wide circular hole in the ground. The Forever Knights dragged Ben and Gwen behind him, leaving Grandpa Max with no choice but to follow.

'Legend has it that The Eternal Pit of Despair is bottomless,' he said. He caught hold of Ben with one hand and dragged him closer to the edge. He grinned wickedly beneath his mask. 'Let's find out!'

With a sudden jerk of his arm, Enoch hurled Ben into the The Eternal Pit of Despair. Screaming in terror, Ben plunged helplessly down into the darkness.

CHAPTER FIVE

THE ALIEN VS THE DEATH GOD

Ben felt his stomach do a flip as he tumbled down the hole. Panicked, he slammed his hand down on the Omnitrix, not sure which alien he had chosen, but certain they all had more chance of surviving than he did.

In a flash of green light, he became the mighty Four Arms. Lucky break. Maybe he'd get out of this yet!

Gritting his teeth, Four Arms dug every one of his fingers deep into the wall of the pit. His powerful grip splintered the rock as he gradually slowed himself down.

After several long seconds, he came to a complete stop. Now all he had to do was climb back out! Steeling himself, he looked up, only to see Gwen and Grandpa plummeting towards him.

Anchoring himself on two hands, Four Arms swang out from the wall. His two free hands found their targets, snatching his grand-father and Gwen from the air as they passed.

They all hung there for a moment, catching their breath. It was Gwen who finally broke the silence.

'Next summer,' she whimpered, 'I am so going to band camp!'

Enoch and a squad of his Forever Knights stood in the chamber of Ek Chuah. They had used the mask to open the doors, and now before them stood a scale model of the temple – a giant, pyramid-like structure, thirty metres high. Right at the very top of the construction, the Sword of Ek Chuah stood silent and still.

'Magnificent,' hissed Enoch. 'Bring it to me!'

The knights nodded and stepped further into the chamber. As they did, a low, rumbling growl echoed from all directions. The villains raised their weapons. Whatever was in there with them didn't sound happy!

✖ ✖ ✖

Four Arms heaved Grandpa out of the pit. The hulking alien clambered up behind him, Gwen clinging tightly to his shoulders.

'Grandpa, I think Gwen needs a second to catch her breath,' he said.

Halfway towards the open chamber doors, Grandpa spun round. 'No can do,' he snapped. 'Enoch may already have the sword.'

'Ever since the alarm went off, that sword is all you think about!'

'You two have to keep your eyes on the prize and remember what's important here!'

'We do remember,' Four Arms replied. 'Do you?'

Before Grandpa could answer, a Forever Knight crashed into the wall next to him. An inhuman howl boomed from within the next chamber, and Grandpa Max rushed over to look.

Slipping from Four Arms' shoulders, Gwen crept after Grandpa, followed close behind by her big red cousin.

Inside the chamber, some kind of giant monster was tossing the other knights around like they were rag dolls. When it spotted the newcomers, the creature screeched with rage.

'It must be Ah Puch,' Grandpa whispered. 'The Mayan God of Death and the Underworld. He's the guardian of the Sword of Ek Chuah.'

'Why can't places like this ever be protected by, like, The Guardian of Cheerfulness?' Gwen groaned. 'Is that too much to ask?'

Ah Puch lifted a struggling Forever Knight into the air, then slammed him down on to a pile of rocks. 'Looks like he's pounding the bad guys for us,' said Four Arms with a shrug.

'Ben, keep him occupied while we get the sword,' instructed Grandpa, creeping over to the stairs that led to the top of the miniature monument.

'Yo, Rat Puke!' the alien bellowed. Ah Puch spun, his red eyes blazing hatred. Four Arms clenched his fists and snarled, 'Come get some!'

Ah Puch covered the distance between them in the blink of an eye. A punch like none he'd ever felt sent Four Arms crashing backwards through a wall. He lashed out with an uppercut, but the monster simply dodged it.

Screeching, Ah Puch brought both fists down on Four Arms, driving the alien down into the rock floor. Again and again the God of Death pummelled his helpless foe, each blow harder and more savage than the one before.

Up on the monument, Grandpa fired a mini grappling hook from the arm of his

Plumber suit. He caught the sword with his first shot, but a bright-blue blade immediately sliced through the rope.

Grandpa Max ducked under a Forever Knight's attack, then stood up quickly, throwing the villain over his shoulder and back down the crumbling stone steps.

Grandpa quickly continued to clamber up towards the sword. Even from this distance, he could feel its power. He had to get to it before Enoch. He *had* to!

Less than a metre from the weapon, he heard Gwen scream his name. He spun round, only to find her some way down the stairs, about to be cut in half by another of the Forever Knights.

Grandpa glanced at the sword. It was the key to either destroying the world, or to saving it. He gritted his teeth. It would have to wait.

Stamping his foot, Grandpa Max kicked the hidden rocket boosters in his boots into action. A burst of flame sent him flying down the steps. He hit the knight like a human battering ram, sending him crashing back down the stairs.

In the corner of the chamber, Four Arms crunched two powerful right hooks into Ah Puch's jaw. The creature howled and flicked out his long, pointed tongue. It wrapped round the alien like a giant snake. With a sudden twist of his misshapen head, Ah Puch whipped Four Arms into the air. The hero barely had time to brace for impact before he was slammed back down against the rocky floor.

Through swollen eyes, Four Arms peered up at the Sword of Ek Chuah. Grandpa and Gwen had made it up there – but so had Enoch! The knight was swinging wildly with his energy sword. Grandpa and Gwen were managing to avoid the attacks, but they couldn't dodge forever.

'No!' gasped the alien as Enoch spun to face Grandpa. His sword was raised, ready to deliver one final, fatal strike.

Four Arms moved his four fists upwards as one, focusing all his strength into a single, devastating blow.

BOOM! The cavern itself seemed to shake when the punch connected with Ah Puch's jaw. The force of the strike sent the monster flipping backwards. Ah Puch squealed in pain as he slammed against the side of the model temple.

The pyramid shuddered, causing Grandpa and Gwen to slide off the top. They landed next to the motionless body of Ah Puch, just as the Ominitrix gave a red flash.

Ben looked down at his human form. 'Ah, not good!'

Grandpa was already powering back up the monument, desperately trying to reach the sword before Enoch could seize it. But the sudden screams of his grandchildren made him stop.

Ah Puch was back on his feet, and advancing towards Ben and Gwen. Without any aliens to call on, they were surely doomed. But the sword! If Enoch got his hands on it, then everyone was doomed. It was the easiest decision Grandpa had ever made.

'Why don't you go back to the barn, birdbrain?' he bellowed, hurling himself on to Ah Puch's back.

Ben and Gwen raced round behind the monster. Together, they slammed their shoulders against the backs of Ah Puch's knees, just as Grandpa leaped clear. Thrown off balance, the death god tumbled all the way to the bottom of the steps. This time he didn't get back up.

The heroes spun, ready to race to the top of the pyramid. They gasped as they realised they were too late. Enoch already had the sword! He cackled as he held the blade aloft.

'At last! The ultimate weapon!' he crowed. 'The world shall kneel before . . .'

He let the rest of the sentence tail off, as the sword crumbled to dust in his hands.

Down below, Grandpa Max blinked, then let rip with a belly laugh of his own. 'I guess that's what happens when your ultimate weapon is five thousand years old,' he chuckled.

Suddenly, the walls of the temple began to shake. Large chunks of rock broke from the roof and smashed against the floor of the chamber. The sword must have been booby trapped. It was time to go!

Panting and wheezing, the Tennysons tumbled through the secret door of the temple. Behind them, the ancient construction collapsed in on itself, trapping Enoch and his knights inside.

'Well,' said Grandpa Max with a grin, wiping the dust from his Plumber suit, 'I could sure go for some dung-beetle stew. It's even better reheated, you know?'

Gwen and Ben looked at each other

and smiled. His jokes might be awful, and his cooking might stink, but it sure was nice to have the old Grandpa back!